ARABIAN HORSES

BILL MUNOZ

DOROTHY HINSHAW PATENT

ARABIAN HORSES

HOLIDAY HOUSE
NEW YORK

Acknowledgments

I wish to thank the following people for the time they spent sharing their love and knowledge of Arabian horses with me: Quita Benton, Simms Arabians, Scottsdale, Arizona; Joe, Pat, and Holly Gervais, Movin On Arabians, Corvallis, Montana; Jane Spahr and Evelyn Sandlas, Ravenwood Ranch, Arlee, Montana; Bob Morin, Mission Arabians, St. Ignatius, Montana; Judy Neely, Desert Jewel Arabians, Hamilton, Montana; Tessa Bradt, North Winds Arabians, Victor, Montana; Walter Sieler, Stevensville, Montana (Morabs).

I also want to thank those who allowed us to take and use photos of them and/or their horses: The Gervais family, pp. 14, 16, 46, 69; Jane Spahr, pp. 2, 8, 11, 35, 41; Bob Morin, pp. 11, 15, 22, 23, 25, 26; Judy Neely, p. 33; Walter Sieler, p. 45; Fred Hartkorn, p. 43; Diane Lemer, p. 51; Jeanette Manley, p. 62; Bill Munoz, p. 38; The Worthington family, Dana Arabian Stud, Roy, Washington, pp. 31, 67.

Library of Congress Cataloging in Publication Data

Patent, Dorothy Hinshaw.
  Arabian horses.

  Bibliography: p.
  Includes index.
SUMMARY: An introduction to the Arabian horse,
a versatile breed noted for its speed, beauty, and
endurance.
    1. Arabian horse—Juvenile literature. [1. Arabian
horse. 2. Horses] I. Title.
SF293.A8P38   636.1'12   81-85090
ISBN 0-8234-0451-X (lib. bdg.)   AACR2

For *Margery Cuyler* and *John Briggs,*
who made this book possible

Contents

ARABIAN HORSES

*Ba Sinhue shows the spirit of the Arabian
as he carries his tail proudly and lifts
his feet high while trotting.* BILL MUNOZ

CHAPTER ONE

Gift of the Desert

THE ARABIAN HORSE IS THE OLDEST BREED OF HORSE IN the world and has been working with people for at least 1,500 years. Arabians are famed for their beauty, speed, and endurance. When horse breeders have wanted to improve their animals, they have bred them to Arabians. For this reason, almost all popular breeds of riding horses have some Arabian blood in them.

Arabian Traits

What makes Arabians so desirable? First of all, their beauty is breathtaking. Even when an Arabian is standing still, it looks proud and alert. Its shiny, thick mane falls naturally on its gracefully arched neck, and its long, silky tail is set high. The Arabian's most beautiful feature is its finely chiseled head. It has a broad forehead between its large, dark eyes. Just below its forehead, the front of its head curves inward, forming its well-known "dished face." Its muzzle is narrow and delicate and ends in a pair of large nostrils and soft lips. Its cheekbones are large and rounded, and its ears are small with tips that curve slightly inward. The Arabian holds its head high above the strong, graceful curve of its neck.

Arabians are small horses. Most are between 14.1 to 15.1 hands tall. (A horse's height is measured in units called hands. One hand is equal to 4 inches. The height is always taken from the ground to the top of the withers, which are the high point of the shoulders. If a horse is said to be 14.1 hands high, that means that it is 14 hands and 1 inch—57 inches—tall at the withers.)

There are practical reasons for the popularity of Arabian horses. Despite their somewhat small size and light build, they are strong. Their bones are denser than those of other horses, so they can carry as much weight as larger horses can. The Arabian has great endurance, too. Its large nostrils enable it to breathe in plenty of air, and it has a big windpipe to carry the air to the generous lungs inside its deep chest. Because it has slender muscles instead of large, bunchy ones, the Arabian can run for long distances without overheating.

The fine head of RG Al Mone shows the dished face, small alert ears, large jawbones, and delicate muzzle of the classic Arabian.
BILL MUNOZ

11

Arabians tend to live longer than other horses, too. Many Arabians are still working and breeding well into their twenties.

Horse of the Desert

A lot of the good Arabian traits are due to the history of the breed. For centuries, Arabians were bred as desert warhorses in the Middle East. Many were raised by the Bedouin tribes that roamed the deserts, traveling from place to place in search of grazing lands for their camels and sheep. Bedouin horses frequently had to go a full day without water. They ate whatever was available, not just grass and grain. Bedouin horses fed often on dates and the milk of camels or sheep. Because of the harsh conditions of their homeland, Arabians had to be hardy and tough.

The Bedouins did a great deal of fighting, and they rode their horses into battle. Each tribesman had his war mare, which was a very special horse. She was like a part of the family and sometimes even lived in her master's tent with her foal. The Bedouins preferred mares because they were gentler than stallions. They were less likely to give away the location of the camp by whinnying when another horse was nearby. Mares were also thought to be hardier than stallions and less sensitive to hunger, thirst, or heat. Many people believe that the modern Arabian horse's friendliness towards humans developed from having lived close to the Bedouins for so many generations. Perhaps the Bedouins did select horses which enjoyed human company and were more likely to stay close to camp.

Bedouins preferred small horses since they ate less than large ones. But the horses still had to be strong to carry their masters into battle. A war mare had to have courage to face a battle without bolting and running. She had to have speed, the skill to stop and start quickly, and stamina to survive and carry her master to victory.

The Arabian "Personality"

One reason Arabian owners treasure their horses is because these animals seem to enjoy human companionship. While many horses walk away when people enter their pasture and need to be lured by a bucket of oats, Arabians often come right up to visitors and enjoy being petted. A journey into the pasture at an Arabian breeding farm can mean a visit from every horse on the place.

The author visits the friendly Arabians belonging to the Gervais family. The only attraction for the horses here is people, and that's enough for them. BILL MUNOZ

Even when they are young, Arabian horses enjoy running. BILL MUNOZ

Arabian horses love to run. If no one is riding them, they may run around the pasture on their own. An Arabian on the move is a beautiful sight, with its arched tail and neck and its flaring nostrils. Because of the Arabian's alertness and love of running, it has a reputation for having high spirits. As a result, some people think that Arabians are hard to control.

But this is not true. Well-trained Arabians are just as easy to manage as any other sort of horse. However, they must be trained with gentleness and patience. Harsh methods and rushing will not work with these sensitive horses. Arabians can be ruined by the wrong sort of training. If they are loved and trained carefully, they become fine companions as well as reliable riding horses.

Holly Gervais plays around with Tezero, the champion stallion she often rides in endurance races. Tezero is a spirited runner, but a gentle playmate as well.
DEBBIE MCKINNEY

This gentle Arabian stallion is a gray which has turned almost white. The foal he is nuzzling is a chestnut.
INTERNATIONAL ARABIAN HORSE ASSOCIATION

Arabian Colors

The most common Arabian colors are bay and gray. A bay horse has a reddish body with black mane, legs, and tail. The body may be light or dark in color. Bays sometimes have white "stockings" on their legs or white markings on their faces. Gray Arabians come in different shades. Many are almost white, with small gray or red spots. Others have a shaded gray color, with the mane, tail, and lower legs darker than the rest of the horse. Gray horses are actually born black and turn lighter as they grow older. A white Arabian is a gray that has grown much lighter with age. Even a light-colored Arabian has dark skin that protects it from the strong desert sun. Only the skin under white markings is pink.

Arabians are sometimes brown or chestnut colored. Unlike a bay, a chestnut horse is the same shade of red all over with no black parts. Browns or chestnuts, like bays, may have white markings. Very few Arabians are black, like the horse in Walter Farley's famous story, *The Black Stallion*.

Some colors are not found in purebred Arabians. An Arabian is never a buckskin (yellow or tan with dark mane, tail, and legs), palomino (golden, with white mane and tail), or pinto (white with blotches of black or brown). These colors often appear, however, in part-Arabian horses.

The Arabs were superstitious about the colors of their horses. Bays were considered hardier and chestnuts, swifter, than other horses. Some sources say blacks were bad luck, but others claim they were thought to be lucky. A horse with a white star on its forehead was considered to be top quality, but if the star was irregular, the horse was thought to bring much bad luck. This was especially true if it had a white "sock" on its right front foot! A horse with three white socks, however, was acceptable, as long as the fourth leg was either the right front or hind one.

One reason Arabians are never pintos or palominos is because the Arabs did not like them. The pinto was called "the brother of the cow," and the palomino was supposed to bring bad luck. Some tribes would not even allow a palomino to spend the night in their camps.

Cass Ole, who played the part of the horse in the film The Black Stallion, *exhibits the spirit, intelligence, beauty, and gentleness of the Arabian.* UNITED ARTISTS CORPORATION

19

An Arabian mare sniffs her new foal as soon
as it is born, before it even dries off.
INTERNATIONAL ARABIAN HORSE ASSOCIATION

CHAPTER TWO

Growing Up Arabian

MOST ARABIAN FOALS ARE BORN IN THE LATE WINTER OR spring. Right from the beginning they have that special Arabian look. Like most horse mothers, Arabian mares take good care of their babies. They let their foals nurse when they are hungry. They do their best to keep their youngsters out of trouble. Arabian mares sometimes have a hard time protecting their foals, since the natural curiosity of the Arabian is especially strong in the babies. When people enter the pasture, the foals are the first to investigate. They come right up for a sniff at the stranger. When a very young foal shows its curiosity in this way, the mother might walk over and put her body between the foal and the stranger. Or if a stallion in a nearby corral shows interest in a filly, a mare might herd her baby away.

A foal's long legs make eating grass a problem. BILL MUNOZ

As the foals grow, they become more and more independent. They begin to eat some grass and to leave their mothers to play together. In the late summer or fall, the foals are weaned. The owners take them away from their mothers so they can't nurse anymore. Usually, two foals are put together to keep each other company while they get used to being independent. The mares are sometimes very sad when the foals are taken away. First-time mothers become especially upset. They may whinny after their foals for days.

But it is important for Arabian foals to learn to be apart from their mothers, since their owners like to sell them soon after weaning. Young Arabians are in demand because people like to buy them as foals and raise them as family horses.

Arabian foals can get to be good friends to one another. BILL MUNOZ

Training an Arabian is different from training some other horses. The Arabian and trainer must be partners. The person teaching an Arabian has to work with it, showing what he or she wants, not forcing anything on the horse. Pat Gervais, a horse trainer who has worked with many horses, including Arabians, says that she never needs to use a whip to get an Arabian's attention. All she has to do is show it what she wants, and the horse cooperates willingly.

Arabians are easy to train since they learn quickly and remember for a long time. Jane Spahr of Ravenwood Ranch fell in love with Arabians when she bought a mare that was seven-eighths Arabian. She had owned several other horses before, none of which were Arabian. The part-Arabian mare was not very expensive, since she had had so little training before being put out in a pasture where she could run free. She had never been ridden, but had learned to wear a halter. No one had handled her for about three years. Her former owner thought she would be hard to work with after being away for so long from people. But Jane found that the mare remembered what little she had learned before, and in three days, the two were partners. Jane was riding a fine, gentle horse that enjoyed being ridden.

The good memory of the Arabian shows in other ways, too. Often Arabians remember human or horse friends after years of separation. They can also remember bad experiences, which can cause trouble with owners. If an Arabian becomes frightened at a particular spot on a trail, it may

Foals learn early to handle their own problems, like scratching an itch. BILL MUNOZ

jump suddenly sideways at that point every time it goes along the trail. It takes a patient person to get around such a problem. The horse must be taken to the place it is afraid of and given plenty of time to investigate. Then it will know that the place is safe.

CHAPTER THREE

Arabians Around the World

THE ARABIANS HAVE A LEGEND ABOUT THE ORIGIN OF THE horse. They say that God created the horse by condensing the south wind. According to Arab tradition, the first man to train horses was Ishmael, who was a son of Abraham and the father of the Arab people. The prophet Muhammad made the horse a sacred animal, and from that time on, breeding and improving the Arabian horse became a religious duty.

In this day of tanks and airplanes, it is hard to imagine how important horses used to be in warfare. But after Muhammad died in 632 A.D., the Muslim warriors conquered the entire Middle East, North Africa, and much of Europe on the backs of their fine Arabian horses. They stayed for centuries and during that time, their horses interbred with European horses and improved them greatly. Even one breed of work-horse, the French Percheron, has Arabian blood that helps make it especially beautiful and spirited.

At a very young age, the head of an Arabian shows its beauty. BILL MUNOZ

After the Europeans became free again, they still admired the Arabian horse. Because the Arabs valued mares so much, the first Arabian horses imported into western countries were stallions. Back then, the Arabs would not sell their mares. Many western horse breeds have an Arabian stallion as the "foundation sire"—the horse that began the breed. One line of the famous Lippizaner horse of Austria can be traced to an Arabian stallion, and all German Haflinger horses trace back to the same Arabian stallion.

Thoroughbred Beginnings

The most important horse to come from Arabian stallions is the Thoroughbred. This breed was developed during the late 1600s and early 1700s in England. In those days, people were not too precise in stating the breed of horses that came from the East, so we cannot be completely certain about some of the Thoroughbred foundation sires. Besides the purebred Arabian, two other breeds from the Near East influenced the Thoroughbred. One of them, the Barb, is a horse from North Africa. The Barb is similar to the Arabian in size and body build, but there are important differences between the two breeds. While the Arabian has a dished face, the Barb has a rounded "Roman nose." The Arabian is famous for its high-set tail, but the Barb's tail is set low. Barbs are even tougher and hardier than Arabians. The other breed which helped father the Thoroughbred is called the Turk, or Turkmen, horse. This breed is tough, lean, and beautiful. Turkmen horses have been raced for centuries. They are fast and can run for long distances.

*The great Thoroughbred mare, Busher, that raced
in the 1940s, had the deep chest, thin "waist,"
and high hindquarters typical of a fast racehorse.*
NEW YORK RACING ASSOCIATION

29

Although many stallions from the East, especially Arabians, were used in developing the Thoroughbred, all Thoroughbreds can be traced back to three of them. The first was called the Byerley Turk. His breeding led to the great racehorse Herod, one of the most important Thoroughbred sires in history. The Darley Arabian was the second foundation sire. His breeding resulted eventually in another magnificent Thoroughbred, Eclipse. The third sire may have been an Arabian or a Barb. Many experts are convinced he was a Barb, but he is commonly called the Godolphin Arabian. The book, *King of the Wind*, by Margaret Henry is about this wonderful horse. He was a very tough animal and lived to be thirty years old, a long life for a horse. His most famous descendant was his grandson, Matchem.

The Thoroughbred horse of today looks very different from an Arabian. It is much bigger—the average size is larger than almost any Arabian ever reaches, about 16.2 hands. Many Thoroughbreds are over 17 hands high. The Thoroughbred head has a straight profile instead of a dished face. But the speed, stamina, and courage of Thoroughbreds remind one of their ancestor, the Arabian.

Raising Arabian horses is popular in many countries. These horses graze contentedly in Washington state. BILL MUNOZ

Arabians in Many Lands

Because of their speed, toughness, and courage, Arabians were especially useful in breeding cavalry horses. This is not surprising, since the Bedouins had used Arabians as war-horses for generations. Poland and Hungary bred Arabian cavalry horses, and they were popular in India as well. In England, the Thoroughbred became the more popular breed, and Arabians were not particularly valued for years.

Then, in the late 1800s, a British couple became interested in breeding Arabian horses. Wilfrid and Anne Blunt traveled over much of the Near East looking for fine Arabians. They were able to buy both stallions and mares. Most were sent back to England where the famous breeding farm, the Crabbet Stud, was established. The Blunts also kept some of their horses at an estate in Egypt.

The mother of this beautiful Arabian stallion,
Supremes Shamrock, comes from English breeding.
BILL MUNOZ

Today, Arabians are very popular in many countries. This is fortunate, since they are bred in only a few places in their native Arabia. The royal families of Saudi Arabia, Jordan, and Bahrain still breed quality Arabians, and Egypt continues to be important as an Arabian breeder. But most of the countries where Arabians are bred are far from the Middle East—Spain, Poland, Russia, Australia, Canada, England, and the United States.

Arabian breeding in different countries has gone on so long that the horses sometimes have quite a different look. For example, Egyptian Arabians are slim and delicate, with especially large eyes, a strikingly dished face, and a flat croup (the top of the hindquarters).

RG Al Mone shows the classic beauty of the pure Egyptian Arabian. BILL MUNOZ

While Polish Arabians share the basic Arabian look with other types, they look sturdier than the Egyptian horses. For many generations, Arabians were bred in Poland for more than just beauty. At the age of three and a half or four, each horse was taken to the track. It was trained to race and was then tested out in races. If the horse was hard to train or became lame, it was not used for breeding. Mean horses, those that got sick easily, or those that had trouble in pregnancy were also discarded. Only the healthiest horses with the best temperaments were allowed to breed. The rest were neutered and sold as pleasure horses.

A lot of Arabians in the United States come from a combination of backgrounds. The first purebred Arabian horses began to arrive in America in the 1700s. Since that time, Arabians have come here from many different countries. Today, hundreds of ranches in America raise purebred Arabians. Many breeders prefer one or another type of Arabian. While some swear by the delicate Egyptian, others are convinced that the elegant Polish Arabian is more appealing. Add to this the people who prefer horses from Russia (where Polish horses are bred with Egyptians) and the lovers of the Spanish strain, and you can see that American Arabians are a varied lot.

*This is Bask, one of the greatest Polish Arabians
ever to come to the United States. Bask won four
U.S. national championships in different events
between 1964 and 1967. His temperament matched his
beauty, since he is said to have been a kind horse.
Bask died in 1979 in his twenties. He sired more
national champions than any other Arabian stallion.*
INTERNATIONAL ARABIAN HORSE ASSOCIATION

CHAPTER FOUR

Part-Arabians

ARABIANS ARE OFTEN CROSSBRED WITH HORSES OF OTHER breeds. The result is called a part-Arabian. Such horses combine the traits of the Arabian with those of the other parent breed and are very popular. With many horse breeds, a part-bred horse can be considered a member of the breed even if it has some ancestors which did not belong to that breed. For example, racing Quarter Horses are often bred to Thoroughbreds to increase their speed. If the half-Thoroughbred horse that results wins enough races, it can be called a Quarter Horse. But Arabians are different. Even a horse which is 31/32 or 63/64 Arabian will never be considered an Arabian; it will always be called a part-Arabian.

This mare is a registered Quarter Horse, a large breed with a lot of muscle. Her foal is half Arabian. Notice the foal's fragile look and dished face. BILL MUNOZ

Part-Arabians can be registered with the International Arabian Horse Association. Then they are called Half-Arabians even if they are more than half Arabian. There are special classes for them at Arabian horse shows. It is very interesting to compare the Half-Arabians to the purebreds. For one thing, the sizes and shapes of the Half-Arabians are more varied than those of the purebreds. Some are pony sized and others are much taller than purebreds. Some have longer bodies or shorter legs than Arabians. But the greatest difference is in color. All the colors that are never found in purebred Arabians can be found in Half-Arabs. There are beautiful palominos, striking Appaloosas, colorful pintos, and elegant buckskins as well as the usual Arabian grays, bays, and chestnuts. Because people have a fondness for one sort of color pattern, many people prefer Half-Arabians to purebreds.

This pinto mare in 15/16 Arabian, and her foal is 31/32 Arabian. Purebred Arabians are never pintos. BILL MUNOZ

New kinds of horses are always being developed to meet different needs, and Arabians are often chosen as a starting point for these breeds. Because Arabians are smaller than many other riding horses, they may be used in breeding ponies for children and small adults. An undersized Arabian is actually little enough to be called a pony. The Pony of the Americas (POA) is a breed developed for children. The POA is a colorful pony, decorated with spots like an Appaloosa horse. To produce the POA, breeders crossed Appaloosas, Shetland Ponies, Welsh Ponies, and Arabians.

The POA is a pony for children developed partly from Arabians. BILL MUNOZ

Another new breed of horse in America has also come from the Arabian. This is the Morab, a cross between a Morgan Horse and an Arabian. The Morab is an all-purpose horse, just like its parent breeds. Morabs have beautiful Arabian-type heads but have stronger-looking bodies like Morgans. Morabs are good horses for endurance rides, for driving in front of a cart, and for working with cattle. Ever since the late 1800s, people have crossed Morgans and Arabians to combine their good traits. But only in 1973 did Morabs become an official breed of horse. To be registered as a Morab, a horse must be at least one fourth Morgan or Arabian, with the other three fourths from the other breed.

The Morab is a new breed made by combining the strength of the Morgan with the elegant beauty of the Arabian. BILL MUNOZ

CHAPTER FIVE

Winners on the Trail

FEW HORSES CAN APPROACH THE ARABIAN FOR ENDURance. Remember that the Bedouins bred Arabians to survive long rides across the hot deserts. Their horses had to be able to make the trip with no problem. In battle, Arabians had to gallop tirelessly for miles or lose their lives. These things helped make the Arabian the toughest, most durable horse around. Because of this ability to travel long and hard distances without difficulty, Arabians are almost always the winners in trail-riding competitions.

Horse and rider teams in trail rides are divided by the weight or age of the rider. There is a junior division for young people, and there are lightweight and heavyweight divisions for adults. The top few finishers in each category win trophies or ribbons.

Holly Gervais with a beautiful foal bred for endurance riding. BILL MUNOZ

There are two types of trail-riding contests. Endurance rides are fifty or a hundred miles long. These races are held often over tough trails. The courses go up steep mountains, down into narrow canyons, and back up again. The first horse across the finish line is the winner, so each rider wants to move as quickly as possible. The horses are raced at a very fast trot or a canter most of the time. However, if the race is close, the last few miles may go by at a faster and faster pace. But speed isn't everything. Every fifteen miles along the way, a veterinarian checks the horses. Each horse must stay at the vet shop until its breathing and pulse drop below a certain level. Then the horse and rider can continue. Some horses must rest for a half hour or more, while others are off and running again in only ten minutes or less. The vet also checks other things to make sure the horse is okay. He examines its legs and hooves for possible lameness problems. By pinching the horse's skin, he can tell if it is in need of water. If the skin flattens back out quickly, the horse is fine. But if the pinched bit of skin stays that way, the horse should drink plenty of water. The vet also checks the horse's gums and eyes for signs of trouble. If he thinks the horse is in bad condition, he can prevent it from continuing the race. Otherwise a foolish rider might harm his or her horse by racing it when it shouldn't be run. If the horse is okay, the vet makes notes about the horse's condition on a card the rider carries. After the race, the cards of the top ten finishers are collected. Judges check the horses again and look over the cards. An award is given for the horse in the best condition and awards are also given for the top finishers.

*Pat Gervais rides her champion stallion,
Tezero, up the trail during the difficult
Tevis Cup endurance ride.* CHARLES BARIEAU

Endurance rides are a challenge for the rider as well as the horse. For a fifty-mile ride, the team is allowed twelve hours to finish. A flat race can be won in under three hours time, but a mountainous ride usually takes from three-and-a-half to four hours to win. Riders have twenty-four hours to complete a hundred-mile race, and some take almost that long. Depending on how hard the course is, fast horses can win in nine hours, but more commonly winners finish in about twelve hours—a long time to be on horseback!

Competitive trail riding is different from endurance racing. These rides are usually forty miles long. Some are run over two days. Then the competitors ride forty miles the first day and twenty miles the second day. The judges are not interested in who crosses the finish line first. Rather, they award prizes to the horses that are in the best condition when they finish. The horses are checked along the way just as in endurance riding, and all the horses are expected to complete the ride in about the same amount of time.

Training for trail riding competition takes a lot of time. The horses must learn to keep up a fast trot for long distances. This is not natural for Arabians, but they learn fast. They gradually build up their endurance, just as a long distance runner does. The rider must be careful not to push the horse too fast and injure it. It takes about three months to get a horse ready for these competitions.

Once the horse is in condition, it can perform every two weeks with no trouble, even if the races are a hundred miles long. A horse can actually race two weekends in a row without becoming overtired if desired. After an event, an endurance horse needs four days of rest to recover from the strain.

This beautiful 7/8 Arabian buckskin and his owner, Diane Lemer, are riding on a competitive trail ride. BILL MUNOZ

During the racing season, many trail riders do not saddle their horses except for the competitions. The rides themselves are enough to keep the horses in shape.

An endurance horse should not have the very flat croup favored in Egyptian Arabians. It needs to get its hind legs under it to go up and down steep, rocky trails. The long muscles of Arabians work better in endurance rides than the bunchy ones of Quarter Horses since the Arabian's muscles cool off faster. Thoroughbreds often make good endurance horses, too. Arabian and Thoroughbred blood can carry more oxygen to the muscles than the blood of other breeds can. This helps the muscles work efficiently. This isn't as true of other breeds. (Remember that Thoroughbreds are partly Arabian in origin). Half-Arabians and Morabs do well in trail riding, also, because of their Arabian background.

Arabian owners in Hamilton, Montana, race their horses at an Arabian show in a friendly contest to see which is fastest. BILL MUNOZ

CHAPTER SIX

Racing Arabians

PEOPLE HAVE ALWAYS TESTED THEIR HORSES TO SEE WHICH are fastest, and the Arabs are no exception. Before the days of the prophet Muhammad, Arab horse races were not especially organized. But Muhammad was very interested in good horses and in racing, so he made rules for the races. Ten horses were enough to make up a race. Trained horses ran a long race by today's standards. It was over four miles. Untrained horses ran about six tenths of a mile. The first seven horses to finish all won money. But the last three won nothing. The top seven were honored inside of a large tent, but the last three were not let in. It was shameful to own one of the last finishers.

Racing Around the World

Thoroughbreds are the most popular racing breed in France, England, and the United States. But in many countries, Arabians are the only horses raced. Arabians have been racing in Spain, India, Greece, Syria, Egypt and Poland for fifty years and more. Arabians are also raced in Russia. In Poland, racing is the biggest test of an Arabian's quality. Even today, a Polish-Arabian stallion must prove himself on the racetrack before being used for breeding. Polish race lengths depend on how old the horses are. Beginning racers run one-mile races, while four-year-olds sometimes run farther than two miles.

Racing in Egypt

Egyptian racehorses are not all pure Arabians. While the British armies were in Arabia, Thoroughbreds came too. Some crossbreeding went on between the two breeds. Now, many racehorses in the Near East have a touch of Thoroughbred blood.

In Egypt, a horse must at least look like a good Arabian to race. The horse is walked in front of a special committee. If the members are not sure that the horse is a pure Arabian, it is galloped for them. By looking at how the horse gallops, they can usually tell if it is pure Arabian. A horse with Thoroughbred blood runs more closely to the ground than a pure Arabian. Because it has a longer back, it can flatten itself out and stretch its hind legs farther under its body. An Arabian, with a shorter back, doesn't reach its hind legs as far under its body, so it gallops higher off the ground.

As horses in Egypt win races, they must again pass inspection by the classifying committee. But these attempts to keep racing horses pure only involve how the horse looks. The horse's parentage is not considered in deciding if it can race or not.

This photo of a racing Thoroughbred named Ancient Title shows that Thoroughbreds, like Arabians, have large nostrils to take in plenty of air when they run.
THOROUGHBRED RACING ASSOCIATION

Arabian Racing in America

In the United States, Arabian racing has only been going on for a few years, but it gets more popular all the time. Arabians are raced in many states, but are especially popular in California, Florida, and Michigan. Arabian races are very similar to Thoroughbred ones. Most are run at distances from five eighths of a mile to one mile. Some of the more important races are from one to one-and-a-half miles.

Although Arabians are smaller than Thoroughbreds, they carry the same weight when racing (110 to 135 pounds). So far, Arabian race winners do not get as much money as Thoroughbred winners. For example, the 1981 International Arabian Horse Association Derby winner won about $20,000, while Thoroughbreds often earn over $100,000 for winning a race. Arabian winning times are also slower than those of Thoroughbreds. But an Arab race is every bit as exciting as a Thoroughbred one, and for people who love the look of the Arabian, such a race is a special thrill.

Saam wins the 1980 International Arabian Horse Association Derby. Notice the legs aren't as long as those of the Thoroughbred.
COURTESY OF DR. SAM HARRISON

57

CHAPTER SEVEN

Showing Off Arabians

ALTHOUGH ARABIANS ARE ESPECIALLY TALENTED AT LONG distance racing, they are also good all-purpose horses. Some horse breeds are bred to be good at just one or two activities. The American Standardbred, for example, is bred only for trotting and pacing races. But Arabians are intelligent and can learn to do different things. At Arabian horse shows, many of these talents are tested.

Aside from the halter classes, which are the beauty contests of horse shows, the most popular events are the pleasure classes. Here a proud owner can ride his or her own horse and show how well trained it is for ordinary riding. The horses are ridden around the ring at different gaits while the judge watches. If a horse misbehaves, it won't win in a pleasure class. The animals are also lined up so the judge can look at each one individually, and each horse must back up on command.

Many different events besides the halter and pleasure classes may be featured at an Arabian horse show. On the following pages are a few examples of how Arabian owners enjoy competing with their horses.

A park horse is also ridden during competition, but it must move elegantly in addition to being beautiful and well behaved. A park horse picks up its feet high when it trots. HERB BYERS

The intelligence and quickness of the Arabian help make it good for cutting cattle. Cutting competitions involve picking out a particular calf from a herd and forcing it out of the group.
JOHNNY JOHNSTON,
INTERNATIONAL ARABIAN HORSE ASSOCIATION

60

The strong bones of Arabians make them good jumping horses.
JOHNNY JOHNSTON, INTERNATIONAL ARABIAN HORSE ASSOCIATION

In dressage, horse and rider work together to achieve precise movements. BILL MUNOZ

The Arabian stallian Ibn T'Chaka is trained in the very difficult art of high school dressage, the sort of work done by the famous Lippizaner horses of Austria.

INTERNATIONAL ARABIAN HORSE ASSOCIATION

63

64

CHAPTER EIGHT

Your Own Arabian Horse

ONE DAY YOU MAY BE LUCKY ENOUGH TO OWN AN Arabian horse. If you are looking for a horse to buy, you should keep some things in mind. As mentioned earlier, Arabian horses are famous for their "spirit." In a good horse, this is a combination of energy plus intelligence. But like any show breed, Arabians have been bred by some people only for looks. Just as there are vicious or high-strung strains of show dogs, so there are flawed Arabians. Many people don't like Arabians for this reason. All they have seen are overbred show animals. They don't realize that most Arabians are gentle horses that enjoy working with people.

The native costume class is one of the favorite events at Arabian shows.
INTERNATIONAL ARABIAN HORSE ASSOCIATION

If you want to buy an Arabian, your best bet is to go to a breeder who uses the horses. Look carefully at the endurance horses. Remember that they must be especially well bred and well trained, since they must be willing and able to carry their riders up and down rocky trails for hours at a time without being disagreeable or easily spooked. Such horses also have sound bodies, because endurance racing tests them to the highest degree.

Other horses to look at are those entered in pleasure classes at horse shows. Winners of these events are selected on the basis of their manners in the show-ring as well as on their beauty. If a rider has trouble controlling a horse, he or she has little chance of winning any ribbons. So if you are considering buying a particular horse, ask about its record as a pleasure horse in the show-ring.

Arabians from racing stock are also worth considering. In order to do well at racing, a horse must first of all be healthy. It must also be able to obey its rider and be used to being around other horses. It will know about riding in a horse van and about being kept confined in a stall. It will also be used to having people pick up its feet and put on its bridle.

If none of these sorts of horses are available, visit local Arabian breeders and talk to them. See what their attitudes are about their horses. Do they think that temperament is important as well as beauty? Do they comment on the disposition of their horses or only on how they look? Go out to the pasture and see the brood mares and foals. Are they friendly?

Remember that good Arabians are very curious, especially when young, and will come right up to you and sniff your hand. Once they have sniffed you, they will usually let you pet them, too, without pulling their heads away suddenly, as long as you don't make any quick movements.

Arabian foals with good breeding love to be around people and share their lives with them.
BILL MUNOZ

Purebred Arabians can be very expensive. If you love the Arabian look but can't afford a purebred, you might consider a part-Arabian horse. Part-Arabians often look very Arabian with lovely dished faces and high-set tails. In either a pure-bred or a part-breed, geldings are usually less expensive than mares and make excellent pleasure horses.

If you do become the proud owner of an Arabian or part-Arabian, you will have found a fine animal friend, and you will be sharing a tradition that is hundreds and hundreds of years old.

Holly Gervais and Tezero take a bareback jaunt through the hills near their home. In 1979, Holly and Tezero won the National Endurance Championship, Junior Division. BILL MUNOZ

Places to Write for More Information

International Arabian Horse Association
224 East Olive Avenue
P.O. Box 4502
Burbank, Ca.   91503

Canadian Arabian Horse Registry
Box 101
Bowden Alta., Canada TOM OKO

World Arabian Horse Organization
Thujas
Bisley, Surrey, GU 24 9AY
United Kingdom

Arabian Horse Trust
3435 So. Yosemite St.
Denver, Co. 80231

Arabian Horse Owners Foundation
4633 E. Broadway, Suite 131
Tucson, Az. 85711

Publications dealing exclusively with Arabian horses:

Arabian Horse Journal
Box 181
Odessa, Mo. 64076

Arabian Express (incorporating *Arabian Racing News*)
Box 845
Coffeyville, Ks.   67337

Arabian Horse Times
R.R. 4
Waseca, Mn. 56093

Arabian Horse World
2650 E. Bayshore Rd.
Palo Alto, Ca. 94303

Arabians West
41945 Fifth St.
Temecula, Ca. 92390

The Arabians
P.O. Box 3
Westland, Mi. 48185

Canadian Arabian News
Box 700
Turner Valley, Alta.
Canada TOL 2AO

Glossary

Appaloosa: A spotted horse developed by the Nez Perce Indians. Some Appaloosas are white with spots all over them. Others have different spot patterns. Many Appaloosas are dark in color with a spotted white "blanket" over the rump.

Barb: An old breed of small desert horse from North Africa. Barbs are very hardy horses. Unlike Arabians, their faces are not dished, and their tails tend to be set low.

bay: One of the most common colors of Arabian horses. The body of a bay is a shade of red, from golden-red to dark mahogany. Its mane, tail, and lower legs are black.

Bedouin: A member of one of the Arabian tribes of desert wanderers. The Bedouins were great breeders of Arabian horses, which they used as mounts in battle.

breed: A particular type of horse which has certain distinctive traits that distinguish it from other horses. Some breeds, such as the Arabian, are very old. Others, like the Morab, are quite new.

brood mare: A mare that is used for breeding purposes rather than for showing or racing. Brood mares can have one foal each year.

bridle: A bridle is made of leather straps connected together to fit over the head of a horse. The bridle also has a metal bit that fits inside the horse's mouth, and reins—long straps leading from the bit to the hands of the rider. The rider uses the reins to control the horse.

buckskin: A buckskin has a tan or yellow body with a black mane, legs, and tail. Many buckskins also have a dark stripe running down their backs.

canter: The canter is a horse's gait between a trot and a gallop.

chestnut: A chestnut has a reddish coat. The mane, tail, and legs are usually the same shade as the body. They may be lighter or occasionally darker but are never black as in the bay.

competitive trail ride: A competition in which horses and riders travel over the same trail in about the same time and judges decide which horses are in the best condition at the end of the ride.

corral: A large, open pen, usually with wooden rails, in which horses or cattle may be kept.

croup: The rear end of the horse above the tail.

cutting competition: A competition to see which horse is best at cutting a particular cow out of a herd and keeping it from returning to the other cows.

dished face: A dished face has a concave (inward-dipping) profile between the eyes and the nostrils.

dressage: A type of training in which a horse learns to respond to commands by its rider given through the reins and rider's legs, telling the horse which foot to put out first, which gait to use, etc.

endurance riding: A competition in which horses and riders cover a long course as quickly as possible.

filly: A young female horse.

foal: A baby horse of either sex.

foundation sire: A stallion to which all or many horses of a particular breed can be traced. Some breeds have several foundation sires (for example, the Thoroughbred) while others have only one (for example, the Morgan).

gelding: A male horse whose testes (organs which produce sperm and male hormones) have been removed. Geldings are generally less excitable than stallions and make excellent riding and work horses.

halter: A combination of leather straps and buckles that fits over a horse's head. The halter allows a person to have some control over a horse, since he or she can hold onto it or snap a lead rope onto it.

halter class: A horse "beauty contest" in which the horses are displayed for looks. They wear only halters and are not ridden in the ring.

hand: The measurement used for the height of a horse. A hand is equal to four inches. The horse's height is measured from the ground to the top of the withers.

high school dressage: Advanced dressage in which the horse does difficult maneuvers at the command of its trainer. The Lippizaner horses are especially bred to excel at high school dressage, but other breeds can learn this difficult art, too.

mare: A female horse.

Morab: A breed of horse produced by crossing Arabians with Morgans.

Morgan: A horse breed which began in the 1700s with the foundation sire, Figure, who was owned by Mr. Justin Morgan. Morgans are small, powerful, versatile horses.

neutered: A neutered animal is one which has had its sex organs removed so it cannot breed.

palomino: A golden horse with a white mane and tail.

park horse: The park horse in a horse show is judged for beauty and for stylish performances at a walk, trot, and canter.

Percheron: A draft (work) horse breed which originated in France. Percherons are the only draft breed with Arabian blood, and their heads are especially beautiful.

pinto: A white horse with black or brown blotches.

pleasure class: Pleasure classes in shows are judged on both beauty and performance. The horses are expected to be well behaved and to obey their riders when asked to walk, trot, canter, or back up.

pony: A small horse less than 14.2 hands high.

purebred: A horse whose parents both belong to the same breed.

register: To list a horse officially with a breed association. When a horse is registered, information such as the names of the parents, the date of birth, color, and any distinctive markings must be listed.

Roman nose: The profile of a Roman-nosed horse is rounded outward instead of being straight or dished.

Shetland Pony: The smallest breed of pony, the Shetland, originated as a work pony in the coal mines of the Shetland Islands.

sire: The male parent.

stallion: A male horse that has not been neutered.

trot: The gait between a walk and a canter. When a horse trots, the front and hind feet on opposite sides move together.

Turkmen horse: An ancient, swift, lightly built breed of horse from the near east (Turkmenistan, now part of the Soviet Union).

wean: To take a young animal away from its mother and feed it something other than its mother's milk.

Welsh Pony: A beautiful pony breed from Wales that is quite popular in the United States.

withers: The highest point on the shoulders of a horse.

Index